MONSTER CRIMES UNIT

CONFIDENTIAL

FRANKENSTEIN'S MONSTER

LAPD

RESTRICTED MATERIAL

AUG 2

OCT 12.84

DEC 11.77

MAR 22.04

THE FRANKENSTEIN JOURNALS

Written by Scott Sonneborn

STONE ARCH BOOKS
a capstone imprint

The Frankenstein Journals
is published by Stone Arch Books,
A Capstone Imprint
1710 Roe Crest Drive
North Mankato, Minnesota 56003
www.capstonepub.com

I dedicate this
journal to my dad.

Text copyright © 2016 Stone Arch Books
Illustrations copyright © Stone Arch Books

Cataloging-in-Publication Data is available on the Library of Congress website.
ISBN: 978-1-4965-0221-6 (library hardcover)
ISBN: 978-1-4965-0365-7 (eBook)

Summary: Fourteen-year old JD is on the hunt — for guts! In this story, the son of
Frankenstein's monster searches for the contributor of his dad's large intestine. The
clues lead him to his cousin, Gloria. Members of Gloria's family have always had one
job: to be a bodyguard to an ancient vampire! But after a run-in with the villainous
Fran, Gloria is wounded after protecting JD. Now the Invisible Man has come to
town to seek revenge on the Vampire, and Gloria is at risk. If JD is going to save
the day and his cousin, he'll need to be brave. Does he have enough guts?

Special thanks to Will, Ben, Ed, Dylan, Zach, and Ms. Prime's Class

Designer: Hilary Wacholz

Illustrated by Timothy Banks

Printed in China.
032015   008866RRDF15

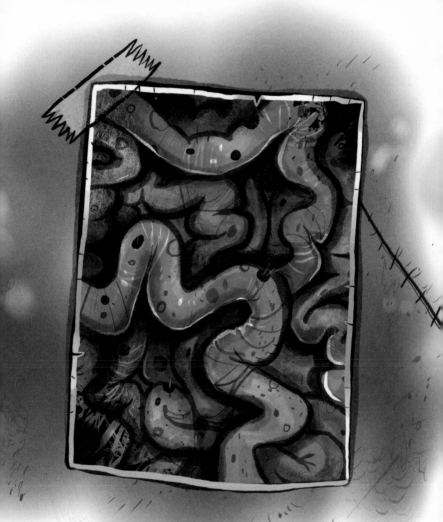

No Guts, No Gloria

Chapter 1

Dear Future Me,

I hope everything's going great for you (meaning me) whenever you're reading this. Because right now, your (my) life has been nothing but crazy since I found Dr. Frankenstein's journal!

Yeah, if you forgot, there were two journals. Mine (this one) that I wrote everything down in so I would never forget everything that's happened.

I only had a few pages of Dr. Frankenstein's journal.

Like the ones where Frankenstein described where he found his monster's brain, eyeballs, and butt. I may not have had all the pages, but I definitely had the grossest ones! But while they did have a lot of disgusting junk in them, they didn't seem to have a ton of clues.

Clues I needed to save my family.

It was still weird to think that I had a big family out there . . . somewhere. Not that long ago I was living in Shelley's Orphanage for Lost and Neglected Children. Back then, I figured I didn't have any family at all. It wasn't until the orphanage went out of business that I found Dr. Frankenstein's journal.

I also found out that I was the son of Frankenstein's monster! I gotta admit — that did kind of freak me.

It also explained why one of my eyes was blue and the other green. Why one of my hands was way bigger than the other. And why my legs were two different sizes.

EEEK!

Body parts from dozens of people went into making my dad. And he had passed down all of their legs, feet, eyes, and hands to me.

All of those people whose parts went into my dad probably had relatives who were still alive. I was related to them too. They were like my cousins!

Cousins I had to find — and fast!

Because if I didn't, Fran Kenstein would get to them first. Fran was the daughter of Dr. Frankenstein, and she had stolen her dad's journal from me (luckily, I had copied a few of the pages first).

With the info she had from Dr. F's journal, Fran planned to use my cousins to build a new monster.

I didn't have anything against monsters. I mean, my dad was one. I had never met him, but I assumed he was a pretty nice guy.

But when I said that Fran planned to use my cousins, what I meant was that she planned to take a hand from one, a leg from another, and so on.

I couldn't let that happen to my family (even if I didn't know who they were). Which meant I had to warn my cousins before Fran could get to them.

But to warn them, I had to find them. That meant figuring out the clues in the pages I did have from Dr. Frankenstein's journal — like this one, about the Monster's large intestine.

Like I said, I may not have had all the pages, but I sure had the grossest ones. This one was full of disgusting pictures, but it didn't have much in the way of clues.

Monster's GUTS

LArge intestine

5 feet long

Boa Constrictor

In fact, it only had a few words on it: "Large Intestine" and "The Monster's Guts." And since "guts" is just another word for large intestine, that didn't really tell me anything at all.

Of course, that wouldn't have stopped Sam.

Sam was my second cousin (the second cousin I had found, that is). His dad was a famous private eye whose actual eye had gone into my dad. Which is kind of gross, but also kind of cool. Because that's what made Sam related to me.

Sam was a police detective in Los Angeles. He'd know where to find clues in Dr. F's journal.

But Sam was still busy wrapping up the case I had helped him solve. Which I totally understood. (If you don't remember why it was so important that the guy we caught stay behind bars, just read the last part of my journal).

Sam didn't even have time to say goodbye. Instead, he gave me something:

My dad's police file from the Los Angeles Police Department Monster Crimes Unit!

I carried it around the corner from the LAPD headquarters, looking for a place to read it. I found a branch of the local library and sat down at a table.

I hoped my dad's file would help me solve the other big mystery in my life: what happened to him? Where did my dad go after he dropped me off at the orphanage and disappeared?

I may have had the eye of a detective, just like Sam, but I couldn't figure this mystery out.

I studied the police file backward and forward. There was some stuff about my dad from before I was born (no crimes, though. I guess he was a pretty good guy). But there was nothing in the file from after I was born.

Still, I hoped there might be some clue about where my dad might be. So my eyes lit up when I saw this:

When I saw that headline, I got excited.

Until I read the article. The monster in it wasn't my dad. It was the Vampire.

Sam once told me, "Just because a clue doesn't tell you everything, doesn't mean it's telling you nothing."

Maybe that was true. But this wasn't even a clue. It was just an old newspaper article that had been put in the wrong Monster Crimes Unit file.

Still, I knew Sam wouldn't just throw the article away. He'd look again to see if there was anything useful in it.

So I took another look. And that's when I saw it!

Under the photo, it said the Vampire's bodyguard had the nickname "The Monster's Guts" — because he was brave and he protected a monster.

I flipped back through the pages I had from Dr. Frankenstein's journal. On the page describing the large intestine, it also said "The Monster's Guts."

MONSTER IN MIAMI

The Vampire, pictured with his bodyguard, Gilford Ennis, Ennis's bravery in the Vampire's service has earned him the nickname "The Monster's Guts."

Maybe Dr. Frankenstein hadn't written that as another way of saying "my monster's large intestine." Maybe it was the nickname of the man the intestine had come from!

That had to be it! That meant the article wasn't misfiled. It had been put in there because my dad got his large intestine from a guy who was the Vampire's bodyguard!

I just might have found where my dad got his guts!

Even better, I figured there was a chance the bodyguard might still be alive. I didn't know much about science or medicine (or a lot of things, really). But I did know that everyone has a large AND a small intestine. You don't need both, right?

Even if my medical knowledge was off, I knew the Vampire was still alive. Or, not alive, but undead or whatever. If a guy like that had kicked the bucket, it would definitely make the news. But I didn't find anything more about the Vampire on the Internet.

Except his email!

So I sent him an email. And he wrote back!

I had a lead on another cousin! Maybe I really did have the eye of a detective.

And the guts of a professional bodyguard!

From: Vamp@Ipingvillage.com

Re: A question about "The Monster's Guts"

Dear sir,

Thank you for your email inquiry. Your suspicions are correct. I would be glad to tell you more in person if you would care to visit me at my home.

Yours,

The Vampire

Chapter 2

A day later, I was in Florida.

The Vampire's email had included a plane ticket. What it hadn't included was answers to any of my questions about his bodyguard. He just said we would talk when I met him at his home.

That turned out to be in a place called Iping Village. It was a retirement community near Miami, Florida.

The one security guard opened the front gate for me. "I bet you're here to see your grandparents," he said. "Go right in!"

I told him I was actually there to meet a cousin, who was related to me through my dad's large intestine.

The guard looked at me like I was crazy.

The Vampire had emailed me the address of his condo. So I started looking for it.

Iping Village was right by the beach, with lots of little houses on a golf course. Every few feet there was a kiosk, or key-ask, or whatever you call those stands that have posters and signs stuck on them.

All of them had signs advertising a show that was playing tonight:

The
IPING VILLAGE
COMMUNITY CENTER
presents
MIMES at 4PM
Get there at 3 for the
EARLY BIRD DINNER

Who wants to see mimes? At four in the afternoon? Or eat dinner at three?

As I walked to the Vampire's condo, I saw the answer: old people.

Iping Village was full of them. Riding on golf carts. Slowly. Very slowly. Or walking — even more slowly — with four-pronged canes.

That's when I had a horrifying thought.

I had been wondering why the Vampire wanted to live in the sunniest place in the entire United States.

Suddenly, it all made sense. All these old people were easy pickings!

I mean, they couldn't move very fast (even on golf carts, their max speed was fifteen miles per hour).

Not to mention, in a place where the average age looked to be ninety years old, it was only natural that some people passed away every year.

If the Vampire got to a few of them early, who would notice?

Then I had an even more terrible thought: why did the Vampire invite me here instead of answering my questions over email? Was it because he was tired of only drinking old people and wanted some fresh blood?! ACK!

Despite the hot Florida sun, a shiver went down my spine. I didn't want to believe a cousin of mine would work for someone as evil as that.

But even if that made my cousin evil too, he didn't deserve what Fran Kenstein had in store for him. I had to warn him.

Without the Vampire getting his fangs in me!

YIKES!

The question was — how was I going to do that?

I had reached the door of the Vampire's condo. As I stood there trying to think, a dog lying outside started barking at me.

It was an old dog. It barely lifted its head to let out a . . .

Woof Woof!

"Hey there," I whispered. "Shhh! I'm trying to figure out how to warn my cousin who I'm related to through his large intestine without being sucked dry by the Vampire!"

It gave me the same look the security guard had. And kept barking.

I had to do something to quiet it down. I closed my eyes and tried to think of what to do.

Only to have someone rush up and tackle me to the ground!

Chapter 3

OOMPH! I hit the ground hard. Holding me down
was a woman who was maybe twenty. Or thirty. It
was hard to tell with her hand pushing my face down.

"Why are you lurking outside the Vampire's condo?"
she asked.

"MRRRMPH," I replied. I was trying to say, "Please
don't feed me to the Vampire!" But it was hard to talk
with her hand on my mouth.

She took her hand off my mouth. "What do you
want with the Vampire?" she asked.

"He invited me here! My name's JD! I just want to talk to him," I cried, "about his bodyguard."

As proof, I pointed to my journal, which had fallen out of my back pocket. The newspaper article about the Vampire's bodyguard was sticking out of it.

"I'm the Vampire's bodyguard," said the woman as she got off of me. The dog hadn't moved but continued to bark at me.

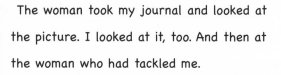

The woman took my journal and looked at the picture. I looked at it, too. And then at the woman who had tackled me.

"You're the Vampire's bodyguard? You look a little shorter now," I said. "And also more like a girl. And also can you get this dog to stop barking? And also . . . didn't the Vampire tell you I was coming?!"

As she studied the picture, she told the dog, "Good boy, Renfield. This is JD."

The dog stopped barking immediately.

"Renfield is the Vampire's dog," the woman explained. "He doesn't move much, but he's an excellent alarm dog. I trained him to bark at anyone he's never seen before. Now that he's met you, JD, he'll never bark at you again."

Then she turned to me. "And yes, the Vampire did say you were coming. But you're not what I was expecting. You have to admit, you do look a bit peculiar."

I nodded. When you have one blue eye and one green, and one hand a lot bigger than the other, you get that a lot.

"Well, anyway, I'm okay," I said, getting to my feet. "I guess it was just a mix-up. No need to apologize."

"You're right," she replied. "That's why I didn't apologize. A bodyguard has to assess every potential risk to her client and act accordingly. I acted accordingly."

She looked at the newspaper photograph of the Vampire and his bodyguard.

"That's my father in the picture," she said. "He was the Vampire's bodyguard. I've got the job now. My name's Gloria."

As she looked at her dad's face in the photo, her mouth turned very slightly in the corners. It took me a second to recognize what her mouth was doing. She was smiling. By the time I figured it out, the tiny smile was gone.

Instead, she was staring at me. Suspiciously.

"And since I'm his bodyguard now," she said coldly, "it's my job to ask: why are you curious about the Vampire's security?"

I told her my whole story, including how Fran Kenstein would be after her because she was my cousin.

I must have talked for ten minutes straight!

She listened carefully the whole time, concentrating on every word.

Finally, when I was done, she said, "Okay, got it."

That wasn't exactly the reaction I was expecting. I sort of thought she'd be surprised to hear about me, my dad, and Fran Kenstein.

It's not exactly your typical fourteen-year-old's life story.

Not to mention, a big part of that story was how her father's guts ended up in my dad!

"I'm sorry to have to tell you about that," I said. "I mean, it's not like it was my fault. Or my dad's fault. But still . . ."

"Don't apologize. You had to tell me that so I could adequately assess the risk Fran Kenstein poses. A bodyguard needs to know the risks to do her job," Gloria said.

"I am not happy to hear about what happened to my father after he died," she said in a tone of voice that didn't sound sad. Or happy. It was all business. "But I don't have time to be sad right now. I have a job to do. The same job my family has always done: keep the Vampire safe while he sleeps during the day like he's doing now."

"That's your family's job?" I asked, confused.

"Protecting the Vampire has always been my family's responsibility," Gloria explained. "In fact, only someone in my family can do it."

"I don't understand," I said.

"Most people don't," she said, handing me a business card. "But a bodyguard doesn't have time to stand around answering everyone's questions about the rules the Vampire lives by. So I made this."

The top of the card read "Vampire FAQ." Below that were all sorts of questions and answers about the Vampire:

Vampire FAQ
(Frequently Annoying Questions)

- Can the Vampire enter a house without being invited?

  Unless it's your own home, entering a house without being invited is breaking and entering. No one can do that under federal law. That includes the Vampire.

- When can the Vampire go outside?

  The Vampire can ONLY go out at night. He will explode if he goes out in the sun.

- So can he go outside on a cloudy day?

  No.

- How about a rainy, cloudy day?

  No!

- How about a day that's —

  NO! He can ONLY go out after sundown.

- Why is your family the only ones who can look after the Vampire?

  The Vampire can only make a pact with one family to be his bodyguard. No one else can protect him.

- Yeah, but why is that?

  Because that's the RULE.

- But what would happen if someone else tries to protect him?

  I don't even want to know the answer to that. So, trust me — if I don't want to know, you don't want to know.

"No one else can protect the Vampire while he sleeps but a member of my family," said Gloria. "My grandfather protected the Vampire. When my grandfather died, my dad became the Vampire's bodyguard.

"When he died, it became my job," said Gloria. "And it's a dangerous job — the Vampire has made a few enemies in the past four hundred years. One in particular."

Gloria looked around.

"Who are you looking for?" I asked.

"No one," she replied. "You can't look for someone you can't see."

I had no idea what that meant. But before I could ask, she turned and looked into my eye (the green one).

"You came here to warn me about the threat posed to my person by Ms. Kenstein," she said. "And you've done that. So please go. I can't afford any distractions while I'm on duty."

She was too busy looking around to even look at me when she said the words.

I didn't know what to say either. Every other cousin I had found had been happy to meet me.

But I guess I had to expect that not all of them would be like that. Still, I had only found three relatives so far. The fact that one wanted me to get lost was pretty disappointing.

Okay, more than disappointing. But whatever. I had a lot more cousins to find and warn about Fran. I had already told Gloria everything she needed to know. Besides, she seemed like she could take care of herself. It wasn't like she needed my help. She had definitely made that clear.

So I said goodbye and headed off to find more cousins who actually wanted me around.

On my way out of Iping Village, I walked across the golf course.

There was one of those kiosks or whatever they're called with a poster for the mime show. It was kind of shady underneath it. Renfield had found his way there (I guess he could move, just really slowly) and was resting in a cool spot.

There was no one else around. It seemed like all the other old people here were kind of like the Vampire and liked to take a long nap during the day.

So I sat there next to Renfield to write down what had happened in my journal.

But as soon as I started, Renfield barked. And barked. It couldn't have been because of me. Gloria had said that Renfield was trained to bark at people he hadn't seen before. But he had already met me.

So I looked up from my journal to find out why Renfield was barking. And saw . . .

Chapter 4

I stared at Fran Kenstein across the eighth hole of the Iping Village golf course.

How could she be here?! She didn't have my dad's police file, and that's what had led me to Gloria.

Apparently, she had the same question for me.

"How are you here?!" asked Fran. "How could you have found out about Gloria before me — when only I have access to all of Dr. Frankenstein's journal?"

That was true. Fran did have all the pages of her father's journal.

But only because she had stolen them from me!

"I guess I shouldn't be surprised," said Fran. "You've already inconvenienced me twice. I thought that framing you and having you arrested would get you out of the way. Apparently not."

She smiled. Which freaked me out. Anything that made Fran happy was not good news for me.

"So I went back to my lab and invented this!" she exclaimed as she pulled out a hair dryer.

"I think someone else already invented the hair dryer," I told her.

"I know that!" she shouted. "I'm a lot smarter than you, after all! Which is why no one else could have transformed an ordinary hair dryer into an AIR FRYER!"

"Um, I think someone invented that too. Isn't an air fryer a thing you can use to cook French fries and fried chicken?" I asked.

Fran turned red.

"Okay, so maybe I need to think of a better name," she admitted. "This Air Fryer doesn't make chicken. It can light air on fire!"

And then she pointed it at me.

"And since you are surrounded by air, that's not good for you." Fran laughed. "It's funny, really — using what used to be a hair dryer to get you out of my hair. Forever!"

I didn't think that was funny at all. I actually found it pretty terrifying. I was so scared, the only part of me I could get to move was my eyelids. I slammed them shut so I wouldn't have to see what was about to happen to me. But I could still hear as Fran shouted, "Goodbye, ughmmmgh!!"

Huh. That wasn't exactly what I expected her last words to me to be.

I risked opening an eye (the green one) and saw Fran on the ground — with Gloria on top of her. She had tackled Fran just like she had tackled me!

Renfield's barking must have brought Gloria running. And just in time! I was safe.

But Gloria wasn't.

"Thank you for saving me the trouble of finding you. You're the one I'm here for," said Fran as her hand reached toward the Air Fryer, which had fallen to the ground.

"Look out, Gloria!" I cried.

Gloria looked confused: "Why? What's she going to do with a hair dry —"

Before I could do anything else, Fran fired! Suddenly, the air burst into flames!

WOOOOOOSH!

Chapter 5

Luckily, Gloria was looking at the Air Fryer when Fran pulled the trigger.

Gloria rolled out of the way just as the air around her caught fire!

The blaze only lasted a second. But that was long enough to melt the bottom of the kiosk advertising tonight's mime show. The heavy kiosk fell over — right on Gloria's legs!

She was hurt. Bad. It didn't look like she could move her legs.

But that didn't stop her from grabbing the Air Fryer out of Fran's hands and aiming it right back at her!

Fran scrambled to her feet and backed away.

"Don't shoot! I'm going!" she cried. She backed away. "After all, I've got plenty more people to visit. Don't I, JD? You won't be able to get to all of them first!"

As Fran ran off, Gloria tried to get up to chase after her. But Gloria couldn't even get to her feet. She stumbled back to the ground.

That's when I realized I had been standing in the same spot the whole time. I hadn't moved at all!

I raced over to Gloria.

"Are you okay?" I asked. "Are you bleeding?"

"I don't have time to bleed," she replied, as she tried to get to her feet again. "I've got a job to do."

It took all the guts I had to look at her legs.

I don't like blood. So it was lucky for both of us that her legs weren't bleeding. But she couldn't stand.

"This is what happens when a bodyguard doesn't assess risks properly," she said as she looked at the Air Fryer in her hands. "I thought this was just a hair dryer. Now I'm too injured to walk."

"I'm sorry," I told her. "This wouldn't have happened if you hadn't saved me."

"Yes, that was another mistake no bodyguard should make," Gloria nodded sadly. "Leaving her client when danger is present."

"Then why'd you do it?" I asked, pretty upset that she had called saving my life a mistake.

"Do you really have to ask, JD?" she said, looking more hurt than when the kiosk fell on her legs.

"Well, yeah," I replied. "I mean, you seemed pretty eager to get rid of me. You said I was just a distraction!"

"I did say you were a distraction," said Gloria. "And I meant it. Being a good bodyguard is very important to me, JD. Because it's what my family does. I care about my job because I care about my family."

She looked at me and added, "And you're family, JD.

"When a bodyguard is on duty," she said, "all she's supposed to care about is her client. Having someone like you around that I care about is a distraction."

"Oh," was all I could think to say.

"Now I have to get back to work," she said, all business again. "Get me over to a golf cart."

There was one sitting nearby next to the golf course. I helped Gloria toward the driver's seat.

"The other side," she told me. "You're going to have to drive. My legs can't work the pedals."

I did what she said and got behind the wheel. It was the first time I had driven anything. Which would have been cool, if it weren't for Gloria.

"Which way to the hospital?" I asked as we drove off.

"No hospital," replied Gloria. "Someone still has to protect the Vampire. Drive me back to his condo — and fast."

I did what she asked, but I didn't like it. Gloria wasn't bleeding or anything, but her legs probably needed casts or bandages or something.

"Can't the Vampire take care of himself?" I asked her. "I mean, he's the Vampire!"

"He is the Vampire," agreed Gloria as we rode on the golf cart. "But think about it. He's four hundred years old. That's old. And like most really old people, he sleeps all day. Sure, in a coffin instead of on the couch. But still. He can't even go outside when the sun is up. Twelve hours out of every day, he's totally vulnerable unless I'm there to protect him."

"If he's so allergic to the sun, why is he living here in Miami, Florida?" I asked. "It doesn't get much sunnier than this!"

"I agree," said Gloria. "I told him he'd be much safer in Alaska or Antarctica or somewhere else that doesn't get much sun. But he wanted to be here, because he likes to be around older people."

Oh man! So I had been right!

"You mean because they won't put up a fight when he sucks their blood!" I exclaimed. "And because no one will be surprised if a ninety-year-old dies in the middle of the night!"

"What? No!" said Gloria. "You have some imagination! The Vampire has been a vegetarian for years."

GROSS!

Huh?! So much for my theory. "But if the Vampire doesn't want to bite them, why does he like old people so much?" I asked.

"The Vampire has lived for a long time," Gloria explained as we crossed the last hole of the golf course. "And like most people who have lived a long time, his favorite memories are from when he was younger. The old people who live here are the only ones who know about the things from the 1940s and 1950s that the Vampire likes to remember. Like Frank Sinatra. And black-and-white movies."

"And mimes," I added, pointing at a poster of the night's mime show as we drove past it.

"Right," she nodded. "I've never seen a mime show. Have you?"

I shook my head no.

"No one under eighty has. That's why the Vampire lives here," said Gloria. "And while I think the sun is an unnecessary risk, there are some things I do like about this place. For one, older people tend to eat very bland food. You won't find any garlic around here. That takes one risk factor out of play. And as a bodyguard, I've got to look out for every risk."

"You make the Vampire sound like a nice guy," I said. "So why does he need a bodyguard?"

"Four hundred years is a long time to live. Even the nicest person is going to make mistakes and rub some people the wrong way," she said. "Or in the Vampire's case, one person."

As she said that, Gloria looked around.

"Who?" I asked. "Who are you looking for?"

"Nobody," she replied. "You can't look out for someone you can't see."

"What do you mean?" I asked.

But Gloria wasn't listening. We were driving past the Iping Village Community Theater.

Gloria was looking at a group of men dressed all in black with white painted faces. The mimes had arrived for their show tonight.

Gloria stared at one of the mimes. Most were tall and skinny. This one was short and fat.

"It's him," whispered Gloria. "He's here!"

Suddenly, the fat mime wiped off his face paint. Underneath wasn't a face. In fact, there wasn't anything there at all!

Even weirder, he started taking off all his clothes!

There was nothing under them either!

I didn't understand what I was seeing (or not seeing).

Gloria did.

"That's the Vampire's archenemy," she told me. "That's the Invisible Man."

Chapter 6

"Drive faster!" cried Gloria. "We've got to get to the Vampire's condo before he does!"

I pushed my foot down as far as it would go, and we raced off.

Well, "raced off" is kind of an exaggeration. I made the golf cart go as fast as it could, but I probably could have run faster.

But Gloria couldn't.

"What's happening?" I asked her. "How did that mime just disappear?"

"That was no mime," said Gloria. "That was the Invisible Man. Remember when I said there was one person the Vampire had rubbed the wrong way? It was the Invisible Man. He must have disguised himself as a mime to get in here with them."

I had never seen anything about the Invisible Man on the Internet. But I guess that kind of made sense. I mean, it's hard to see a lot about someone you can't see.

"He's been trying to get revenge on the Vampire for years," said Gloria. "My family has always stopped him."

"What did the Vampire do to him?" I asked.

Gloria wasn't sure exactly. It had something to do with the Invisible Woman. But whatever it was happened years ago. The Vampire hadn't seen the Invisible Woman in a long time.

"Well, he never actually SAW her," said Gloria. "She is invisible. But, they were dating behind the Invisible Man's back. Or maybe in front of his back too. It's kind of hard to tell with invisible people."

"That sounds kind of complicated," I said.

"Not for me," Gloria replied. "When you're a bodyguard, everything is simple. It all comes down to doing whatever it takes to keep your client safe."

We pulled up in front of the Vampire's condo. I helped Gloria inside.

In the living room, where the couch should have been, was a coffin. A huge coffin. It looked like it weighed a ton (or maybe ten tons? How much is a ton? Anyway, it must have weighed a lot).

"Whoa!" I said. "Is the Vampire . . ."

"Yes," replied Gloria as she went to the coffin. "The Vampire is safe in there. For now. The coffin can only be opened from the inside. Unless you have this."

She pressed the side of the coffin. A panel popped open. Gloria took out the key that was hidden inside.

"The coffin is indestructible," she explained to me carefully. "The Invisible Man knows he won't be able to get inside and get his revenge unless he has this key."

"So why'd you just take the key out of its hiding place?" I asked.

"The Invisible Man knows all about the key and the coffin," she replied. "He and the Vampire used to be good friends, remember?"

"Okay, so let's use that key and get the Vampire out of here!" I said.

Gloria looked out through the window. "There's still some time until sundown," she said. "Taking him out of his coffin now would destroy him."

One thing was for sure — we weren't going to move the Vampire inside the coffin. Whatever made it indestructible also made it incredibly heavy.

OUCH!

"I can't fight the Invisible Man," said Gloria as she took some bandages from the Vampire's bathroom and wrapped up her legs. "And I won't be quick enough to keep the key away from him either."

"Don't panic," I told her. "I'll figure something out."

That's what I always said when I found myself in trouble. Sometimes, I said it to pump myself up without totally believing it.

This time, I didn't believe it at all. But Gloria seemed to. She wasn't panicking at all.

"That's correct. You are going to have to figure it out, JD," she said. "Because you're the only one who can."

Gloria held up the key.

"According the Vampire's rules, only a member of my family can protect him," she said.

I started to ask "why," but Gloria held up her card. The one with the "Annoying Vampire Questions."

"I don't have time to explain the Vampire's rules on a normal day," she said. "And this is not a normal day. You're the only one who can do this. But I promised to protect the Vampire. It's what our family has always done."

I was part of that family. I was the only one who could help her. There was just one problem.

"I don't how to be a bodyguard!" I said.

"All it takes," Gloria told me, "is everything. You have to be willing to do everything you can to make sure nothing happens to the person you're protecting."

She turned and looked me in the eye (the blue one this time). "The only question is," she said, "do you have enough guts?"

I knew the answer immediately. Of course, I didn't have the guts!

Chapter 7

I was scared out of my mind. How could Gloria and I be related? Nothing scared her! She had way more guts than I did!

But then I remembered that the guts she had were inherited from her dad. Which meant they were in me too — because they had been in my dad.

She was family. And now that I'd found her, I didn't want to lose her. Which maybe I would, if she tried to protect the Vampire on her own without being able to use her legs.

"Give me the key," I told her. "If you think I can keep it away from that invisible guy, I'll try my best."

"I never said I thought you could keep it away from him," said Gloria, handing me the key. "I believe the risk is lower with you. I estimate that giving you the key reduces the risk to my client by twenty percent."

"Whoa — wait!" I exclaimed. "So you're saying I've only got a twenty percent chance of getting out of here without some crazed guy I can't even see grabbing me!?!?"

WHAT????

"No," replied Gloria calmly. "I estimate my odds of evading the Invisible Man with two injured legs are approximately five percent. Giving you the key increases my client's odds by twenty percent. In other words, you have a six percent chance of success."

"Oh," was all I could think to say — before a crashing sound made both of us turn our heads toward the door.

BOOM!!!

"The Invisible Man is coming," said Gloria evenly. "Your odds are dropping by the second. I suggest you go. Now."

The door swung open like it had been kicked in. But no one was there.

Gloria moved to block the door — only to fly off her feet. She hung there, a yard off the ground.

"Where is the key?" demanded the Invisible Man. "Tell me quick. I grow tired of holding you aloft."

"Put her down!" I shouted. "I have it!"

"JD, don't," said Gloria, raising her voice for the first time. "This isn't about me!"

It was for me. But I didn't stand around to argue with her. I took off running. And hoped the Invisible Man followed.

I looked over my shoulder and saw Gloria fall to the ground. She was okay.

But somewhere between me and her was the Invisible Man.

I was glad I had gotten him to leave Gloria without hurting her.

Now I just had to make sure he didn't hurt me!

I raced to a window, pushed it open, and jumped outside.

I hit the ground and started running.

I had two choices: find a way to fight the Invisible Man or find a place to hide.

I guess that might have been a tough decision for some people.

For me, it was easy. Of course I was going to hide!

I made a loop around the Vampire's condo and opened the door to the nearest building.

It was the small community library with books and board games. Inside, it was dark and empty.

I closed the door quietly behind me, then risked a peek out the window.

I didn't see anything. Nothing at all.

Not even the Invisible Man's face, which was right there staring back at me!

Chapter 8

Of course, I only realized that when — CRASH! —
the window smashed in on me.

I could feel a hand grabbing at me. But I couldn't
see it. I could only smell the hint of sweat as the
Invisible Man struggled to reach me.

I backed away from the broken window.

"I grow weary of this chase," wheezed the Invisible
Man, slightly out of breath. "Give me the key."

Suddenly, a couch floated up and came flying at me.
And then a table and a chair.

I dodged the first two. But the chair hit me and bruised my arm numb.

That's when something else hit me too: the furniture wasn't flying on its own. The Invisible Man was throwing it!

Another chair (a really big one) levitated into the air. But instead of flying at me, it was smashed to pieces.

The message was clear. If the Invisible Man got his hands on me, the same thing would happen to me!

I crept back into the shadows of the darkened library and tried to hide behind a shelf of books.

I was definitely proving how much guts I had.

None.

Then suddenly, I heard a . . .

CREEEEEEEAK.

It was the bookshelf I was hiding behind. The Invisible Man was right there on the other side, trying to topple it on me!

"**URRH!**" he groaned as he shoved. He was so close that I could smell his sweat as he pushed hard.

The shelf was so overloaded with books, it took him maybe three seconds of pushing to get it to fall over. Which was just enough time for me to scramble out of the way, as **WHOOMP!** it crashed to the floor.

The Invisible Man had to climb over the fallen shelf, giving me time to run out of the library.

I had to find somewhere else to hide. If he could get that close without me knowing, there's no way I'd escape if he found me again.

Outside, I ran past Renfield, sleeping on the grass.

He lifted his head an inch above the ground and let out a loud **WOOOOOF!**

"Shh!" I pleaded. "I need to hide. I know it's not what Gloria would do, but I'm kind of new at trying to be brave and —"

I stopped trying to justify myself to a dog when I realized Renfield wasn't barking at me. Only there wasn't anyone else around. Renfield must have been barking at the Invisible Man!

Gloria had said she'd trained Renfield to bark at anyone he hadn't seen before. Well, there was no way Renfield had ever seen the Invisible Man!

But Renfield could smell him. I took off in the opposite direction, silently reminding myself to thank the old dog, if (I meant "when" — stay positive!) I survived all this.

And I really did need to thank him. Not only had Renfield's bark warned me the Invisible Man was close (it sure would have been great if Renfield could move fast enough to stay with me as I ran) — he had also given me an idea.

Renfield had smelled the Invisible Man. I had, too, when he was close enough to grab me. He was certainly working up quite a sweat chasing after me.

I remembered that when he was dressed as a mime, he kind of stood out as being overweight. Which I guess made sense: if you're invisible, you don't have any motivation to go to the gym to try to look good.

If he were out of shape, then the more I could make him run, the sweatier he would get. Maybe I could get him so sweaty, I could smell his BO coming. I could use my nose instead of my eyes!

I wasn't sure that was a great plan.

In fact, I hoped it really stank!

Chapter 9

I ran for a long time.

That's really all there is to say.

I ran and thought about what the Invisible Man had done to that chair — and hoped he didn't get the chance to do that to me.

* * *

I must have run for hours. I ran past the theater, all over the golf course, and around the condos. I don't know how many laps I made of Iping Village.

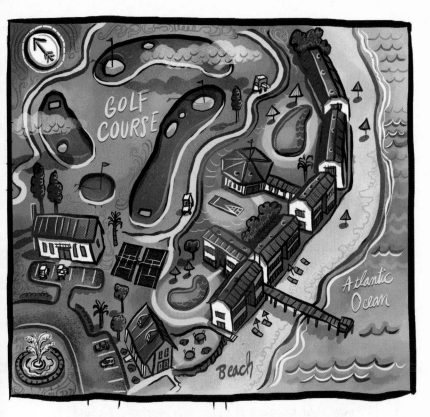

ILPING VILLAGE

I kind of lost track of time. It was actually kind
of boring. Or would have been if I wasn't completely
scared out of my mind.

Of course, it would have been easier if I could have just run out of Iping Village and gone somewhere (anywhere) else.

But one whole side of the place ended at the beach. I guess I could have tried to swim for it. But I was staying ahead of the Invisible Man by running. I didn't know if he'd be faster than me in the water.

The rest of Iping Village was surrounded by a huge fence. There was only one gate. I ran by it a bunch of times, but the security guard had it closed. I never had time to stop and explain why he should open it for me, because the Invisible Man was right behind me.

PEWW!

I knew that because my plan was working. I could smell his BO a mile away.

Okay, maybe not a mile. But far enough that I had time to run in a different direction when I smelled him coming too close.

As long as I could keep this up, I could keep the key away from him.

There were just a couple problems with doing that. One: it was kind of embarrassing.

None of the old folks were outside to see me. I guessed they were all still taking their afternoon naps, just like the Vampire.

The only people outside were the mimes, who were holding up the clothes the Invisible Man had been disguised in. They seemed totally surprised that one of them had just disappeared and were trying to tell the security guard what happened.

Well, they weren't exactly trying to tell him. I guess they took their miming — or whatever you call it — very seriously. They didn't say a word. They just flapped their arms and waved their hands.

I guess I can't really blame the guard for looking at them like they were crazy. I must have looked even crazier to him every time I ran past him as I made my loop of Iping Village. I was running for my life, but he couldn't tell anyone was chasing me.

So I'm sure I looked like a crazy person.

I mean, I am literally sure. Because each time I ran past him, the guard yelled, "What are you doing!?! Are you crazy!?"

Like I said, I didn't have time to explain that I wasn't crazy (not that he would have believed me) because the Invisible Man was right behind.

And anyway, I could handle a little embarrassment.

What I couldn't handle was all the running. One of my legs was shorter than the other, and both of my feet were super huge. That made running hard.

I was getting tired. Really tired. Pretty soon, I'd have to stop.

Which, on the one hand, would be good. At least I'd stop embarrassing myself in front of the guard.

On the other hand, the Invisible Man would catch me, get the key, and do who knows what to the Vampire.

Not to mention me.

I ran out of steam as I was passing the security guard for the nineteenth time.

My legs just wouldn't run anymore. I pitched forward and collapsed.

Right onto the golf cart next to the security guard!

I hopped in and drove off!

"What're you doing?! Are you crazy?" cried the guard again. "That's my cart. Stop!"

The mimes all stuck out their palms at me, echoing his calls to stop.

But I didn't listen. (Can you "listen" to people who aren't talking? That sounded like a question I should ask the guy I couldn't see. Which I would have if he weren't trying to smash me.)

The security guard hopped onto another golf cart and chased after me.

As he pulled up alongside, I finally had the chance to explain to him how I was being chased by the Invisible Man who wanted the key to the Vampire's coffin that I had gotten from my cousin who was related to me through my dad's large intestine.

Even as I said it, I knew it made no sense.

The guard seemed to agree. "You really are crazy!" he said.

And then he flew out of his golf cart and landed on the ground.

"Hey, who did that?" said the guard as he stumbled to his feet.

I already knew the answer — the Invisible Man.

He got behind the wheel of the guard's golf cart and chased after me. Slowly. Very slowly.

I could have gotten out and run faster than we were driving.

But I was too tired to run.

Luckily, so was the Invisible Man.

I could hear him wheezing in his cart. He was too busy catching his breath to say anything as he chased me across Iping Village.

And then suddenly I stopped.

VRRRRRR! My golf cart's wheels kicked up sand. I had taken a wrong turn and gotten stuck on the beach!

Having run all over Iping nineteen times, I guess I should have known the place better. But it was starting to get dark and I was too busy being scared out of my mind to really watch where I was going.

The Invisible Man followed me onto the beach and got his cart stuck too. But that didn't stop him. I could see his footprints coming toward me in the sand.

Hey, wait! I could see his footprints in the sand!

I hopped off my cart and ran across the beach. I had gotten a bit of rest while driving the golf cart. Enough to run a little more.

And I knew where to run because I could see the Invisible Man's footprints under the now-setting sun. So I knew where he was!

Unfortunately, it wasn't long before the Invisible Man figured that out. He ran straight into the surf (I guess he had caught his breath too).

The waves were breaking hard. I couldn't tell where he was in the water.

Even worse — the ocean water was like a bath. Now I couldn't smell him either!

And even even worse — the sun was going down. It was getting darker.

And even even even worse — well, no. That was as bad as it got. But that was bad enough!

The Invisible Man could have been anywhere. I couldn't smell him. I couldn't see him. It was so dark I couldn't see anything.

Until the air lit up on fire!

"JD! Over here!" said Gloria. She was in another cart at the edge of the sand. She fired another burst from the Air Fryer that lit up the beach.

I saw footprints in the sand. The Invisible Man was coming for me.

And then, just as the flames from the Air Fryer died away, I saw something else.

Next to Gloria, there was someone behind the wheel of the cart. In the dim moonlight, it was too hard for me to see who it was.

Until he rushed right past me, and I saw . . .

The Vampire!

"No," cried the Invisible Man. "I was going to have my revenge!"

"Yes, you vere," said the Vampire, in whatever kind of weird accent the Vampire had. "But dees boy made you vait too long. It ees now night. Too late vor you!"

I really couldn't see what happened next. Between the Vampire's black cape and the Invisible Man being invisible, I couldn't tell what the two were doing in the darkening night.

I heard a "Hrnnn!" and then a "Ommph!" and then "**SCRREEECH!**" and then a "**SHOOPH!**" that might have been a hiss of smoke. And then the Vampire and the Invisible Man were gone!

COOL!

Chapter 10

The next morning, I woke up in the Vampire's condo.

No, not in his casket.

Gloria had invited me to sleep on the couch. As I slid off it, both my legs burned from all the running I had done the day before. But I couldn't complain about my legs. Gloria had new casts on both of hers.

It would take a little time for them to get better, but that was okay. She had time.

Whatever had happened to the Invisible Man (Gloria wouldn't tell me), he wouldn't be back for a while.

In the meantime, she could get around Iping Village on a golf cart.

I offered to stay and help her, but she told me no. I understood. "I guess I showed yesterday how much help I would be to a bodyguard," I said. "I mean, when things got scary, all I could think to do was run or hide! "

"That's right, JD," she replied. "You did show how much help you could be last night. And all you did was . . . save my client!

"What you did last night was the bravest thing I've ever seen," she said. "I told you that you only had a six percent chance of success, and you agreed to help anyway. Being brave doesn't mean you're never scared. It means that even when things are scary, you still agree to take on the jobs that need to get done.

"You're exactly the kind of person whose help I could use, JD," she said.

"Oh," was all I could think to say. "Thank you."

"You shouldn't be so surprised," said Gloria. "We both got our guts from my father. He was the bravest man I ever knew.

"But I can't let you stay, JD," she went on. "Because you've got another scary job that needs doing. You've got to warn the rest of your cousins about Fran. Now that I know what she looks like, her risk to me is somewhere between low and minimal. Your other cousins are at a much higher risk, if you don't get to them first."

She handed me a bag. After I had fallen asleep on the couch, the Vampire had returned. He had taken the key from my pocket, but before he got back in his casket (I guess he was in there right now!), he had left the bag with Gloria to give to me.

"He wanted to give you a little something to thank you for helping keep him safe," she said.

The bag may have been little, but it sure was something. Inside were a handful of gold coins!

"Whoa," I said. "These look old. Are they from the last century?"

"Try three centuries before that," she told me. "They should be worth enough to get you wherever you need to go to find your next dozen cousins."

Tracking down my first three cousins hadn't been easy. Thinking about what it would take to find the next twelve filled me with a gust of fear. It sure would have been easier with Gloria's help. But she had a job to do.

So did I. And with the gold coins in one back pocket and my journal in the other, I headed out to do it!

THE END?

GLOSSARY

archenemy (arch-EN-uh-mee) — one's principle or worst foe

condo (KON-doh) — an apartment house or other development in which each unit is owned by the person who lives in it

kiosk (KEE-osk) — a small light structure with one or more open sides used especially to sell merchandise or service

levitated (LEV-i-tay-tuhd) — to rise or cause to rise in the air in seeming defiance of gravity

orphanage (OR-fuh-nij) — a place where children who don't have parents live and are looked after

mime (MIME) — a performer who expresses himself or herself without words

revenge (ri-VENG) — action that you take to pay someone back for harm that the person has done to you or someone you care about

NOT AS SCARY AS HE LOOKS!

Scott Sonneborn has written dozens of books, one circus (for Ringling Bros. and Barnum & Bailey), and a bunch of TV shows. He's been nominated for one Emmy and spent three very cool years working at DC Comics. He lives in Los Angeles with his wife and their two sons.

COOLEST ILLUSTRATOR EVER!

Timothy Banks is an award-winning illustrator known for his ability to create magically quirky illustrations for kids and adults. He has a Master of Fine Arts degree in Illustration from the Savannah College of Art & Design, and he also teaches fledgling art students in his spare time. Timothy lives in Charleston, SC, with his wonderful wife, two beautiful daughters, and two crazy pugs.

Find a **MONSTER** load of fun at...

WWW.CAPSTONEKIDS.COM

SUPER COOL STUFF!!!

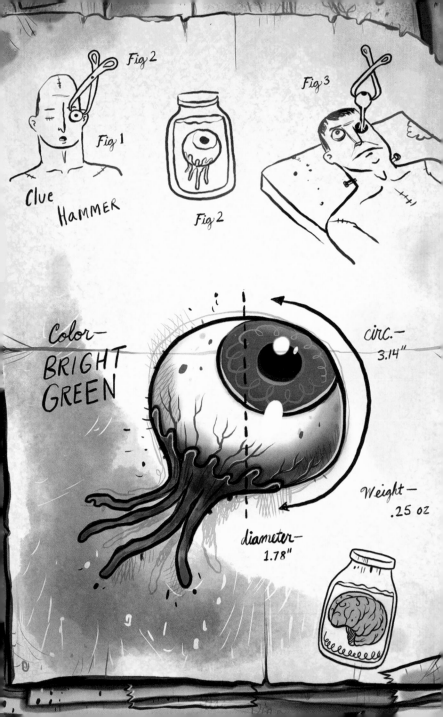